The Kitten Psychologist And The Kitten Come To A Conclusion

THEA VAN DIEPEN

OTHER WORKS

Find other works by the author at
https://www.theavandiepen.com

The Kitten Psychologist And The Kitten Come To A Conclusion

INKLETS #18

THEA VAN DIEPEN

Inkprint PRESS

www.inkprintpress.com

ISBN: 978-1-925825-17-6
eBook ISBN: 9781386990062

www.inkprintpress.com

*National Library of Australia Cataloguing-in-Publication
Data*
Van Diepen, Thea
The Kitten Psychologist And The Kitten Come To
A Conclusion
28 p.
ISBN: 978-1-925825-17-6
Inkprint Press, Canberra, Australia
1. Fiction—Animals 2. Fiction—Short Stories

First Print Edition: September 2019
Cover design © Inkprint Press
Interior art © Amy Laurens

THE KITTEN PSYCHOLOGIST AND THE KITTEN COME TO A CONCLUSION

Bოth Worn Jeans and Green Shirt looked at me.

"Well, I have been having a hard time getting patients." I said. "How did you know?"

"You told me about it. Before you knew I was sentient. And you'd told everyone else about it just before then, if not so bluntly as you did me." The kitten glared at its owners. "What else did you think all those tales of financial woe were about? So, since you nodded and listened and did nothing to help, I decided to do so. After all, I had problems, and here was a psychologist in need of patients. You would have paid for the sessions if it had been your idea."

I vaguely recalled that day—it had been at a party. Unfortunately, I'd been so down I'd had a little too much to drink to remember details.

"So you do have a heart," I said. My friends bristled, but the kitten gave me a wry smile.

"I wasn't about to let you know that. I am a cat. But," it sighed, "it appears circumstances have forced me to reveal myself. Don't go telling any-one."

"I'd thought you were just being down on yourself," Worn Jeans said to me.

"How are you paying for this office?" Green Shirt asked.

"Weren't we here to talk about..." I waved my hands in their general vicinity. To tell the truth, I was embarrassed to admit that the only way I'd been able to afford the office for the past year or so was by subsisting off of less-than-stellar food. Which hadn't helped my emotional state, that was for sure. "Was this only about the bank, or is there more?"

"Well, clearly there's more," remarked Worn Jeans.

And then proceeded to say nothing more.

"Ah, yes, well." The kitten cleared its throat. "I went to more than the bank."

"You what?" said both my friends in aghast chorus.

The kitten ignored them and addressed me instead. "Have you heard of the cat cafe that opened up in our neighbourhood?"

"The Cat's Paws?"

"Take a Paws. Yes. They're... willing to give me a job. If I have a bank account so they can deposit my pay-cheques."

My friends and I all sat back. Hadn't the kitten lectured me at length about the unfeasibility of kittens getting jobs? In great detail? Over Skype and email? Without giving me a chance to say much more than three words in a row?

"What will you be doing?" asked Green Shirt.

"Roaming their establishment, entertaining their customers by virtue of being feline. In return, they would provide me the means with which to pay off the debt I have incurred and, afterwards, continue to make use of this fine psychologist's knowledge and experience."

"Provided everything you do is your idea," I said, a little dazed at being called a fine psychologist.

"Precisely. I do have my dignity to maintain."

"And that's why you went to the bank," said Worn Jeans, as though not quite sure to believe these words.

The kitten nodded.

"You did all of this to help our friend?" asked Green Shirt.

Oh. Wow. I hadn't even thought of that.

"A friend who did everything possible to help all of us when my first strategy fell apart."

"So what do we do now?" asked Green Shirt, but not of me. Of the kitten.

Worn Jeans had also turned away from me and to the young cat.

The kitten, in turn, drew back and gave me a pleading stare.

Be honest, I mouthed.

The kitten's head drooped, but only for a moment. It took a breath, drew itself up, and said, with the kind of poise only a cat can have: "I cannot do this by myself. Will you help me?"

Maybe one day, the kitten won't need a psychologist. Maybe one day, I won't need a kitten. That's what I'd thought more times than I could count ever since I decided to grow a conscience.

But, before I left my office on Wednesday with my friendships intact and the kitten, impatient, already gone outside, I paused a minute with Worn Jeans and Green Shirt.

"It's hard to think it was scared of going outside when it first spoke with you," said Worn Jeans. "I wish we'd known, but it looks like you really helped."

I guess I did.

"Will our kitten's visits be enough to help you keep afloat?"

"Not really, but it's better than nothing."

"Anything we can do?" asked Green Shirt.

I considered.

Referrals would be great, but how awkward was it to tell your friends to go to a psychologist?

Probably no more awkward than telling them their cat was sentient.

"Let your kitten make its own choices," I said. "And if you hear of anyone needing a psychologist, send them my way."

"What if those people include us?" asked Worn Jeans.

"Just make sure you pay me," I said, with a bit of a forced chuckle. My friends smiled, but I remembered our previous sessions. "How about, for now, let's focus on being friends for a while. I've been moping around by myself long enough."

"Sounds good to me," said Worn Jeans. "Want to come over for dinner tomorrow?"

"That sounds amazing. I've… uh… been having a lot of Kraft Dinner lately." I paused. Did I want to leave the reason in the blanks for them to fill in? But I supposed that, for all the talking we'd done, it was the things we hadn't said that had led to all this trouble in the first place. "For the last year, actually. That's how long my finances have been this tight."

"Then," said Green Shirt, putting a hand on my shoulder. "Come over as often as you like."

There once was a little kitten who had decided that the outside was bad. One hundred percent, unequivocally, without question or shadow of a doubt dangerous. And yet, one day, outside it went.

Now the time had come for its psychologist to go outside, too.

And, once my friends and the kitten had left the building, that's exactly what I did.

THE MAKING OF
THE KITTEN PSYCHOLOGIST AND THE KITTEN COME TO A CONCLUSION

As I was writing what I knew was the last part of this story, I felt this nudge to go back to the beginning. Why did the kitten need help to begin with? What good had that done, both for the kitten and the psychologist? And how did those initial circumstances tie in with the ending, anyways?

The thing about writing what you thought would be a silly one-off, and then deciding later you'd write a series, means that the whole thing feels so... random. I'd worried whether the first part of the story even made sense as part of the series, or if it was this odd part, hanging out with the rest so their existence could be justified.

So, as the bomb of the kitten having a conscience had dropped and the aftermath played out, I was taking a whole new look at what had really happened leading up to and during that kitten's first session with the psychologist.

Because if this had happened that way, then really... really.

And then I found the first lines of the story going through my head again, and I understood.

The story had never been about the kitten.

It had been about the psychologist.

I'd started writing these stories with the psychologist as a humorous, semi self-insert, to help this kitten through the problem I'd personally been having with stepping out. And, as it turns out, when you write a series of stories as therapy sessions for yourself, the story's not over until the character you've really based on yourself gets the help you've been needing.

Funny how that works.

(P.S. I really want a cat cafe called Take a Paws to be a thing irl. Someone, go do that.)

READ MORE!

DREAMING OF HER AND OTHER STORIES

A collection of short stories and poetry, written as refreshers, reminders of what makes life beautiful. Pieces include a story of the life of a river as he discovers his true self, a poetic retelling of Daphne's flight from Apollo, and, in the titular story, a literal nightmare as a girl comes to terms with the death of her sister.

https://www.theavandiepen.com

ABOUT THE AUTHOR

THEA VAN DIEPEN spent the first ten years of her life on a tree-wrapped acreage where an inquisitive child might believe in magic. Nowadays, she lives in Edmonton, breathing life into stories in the form of books such as the *White Changeling* series, a webcomic, and a video game.

Her website is theavandiepen.com, where she can be contacted in English and French... so long as you don't ask her to count in French, as she tends to miss numbers ending in six entirely by accident.

INKLET #007
SEVENTY
LIANA BROOKS

INKLET #008
A Final Request
for Mercy
AMY LAURENS

INKLET #009
the kitten psychologist
vs.
the kitten's owners
THEA VAN DIEPEN

INKLET #010
Answer the
Question
AMY LAURENS

INKLET #011
Happily,
Red
AMY LAURENS

INKLET #012
the kitten psychologist
tries to be patient
through email
THEA VAN DIEPEN

INKLET #013
DRAGON
Tuesday
AMY LAURENS

INKLET #014
RED PLANET
REFUGEES
LIANA BROOKS

INKLET #015
the kitten psychologist &
What The Kitten Did
THEA VAN DIEPEN

INKLET #016
Cherry Blossom
AMY LAURENS

Alone
AMY LAURENS

the kitten psychologist & The Kitten Come To A Conclusion
THEA VAN DIEPEN

LEVEL NINE
LIANA BROOKS

INKLET #020
To Dust
AMY LAURENS

INKLET #021
Interchange
AMY LAURENS

INKLET #022
Emalia's Lanterns
LIANA BROOKS

INKLET #023
Dear Santa
AMY LAURENS

INKLET #024
The Quilt-Maker's Scrap
AMY L. LAURENS

www.ingramcontent.com/pod-product-compliance
Lightning Source LLC
Chambersburg PA
CBHW051303190726
48286CB00004B/1247